UNICORN ACADEMY
...Where magic happens!

There was a flash of pink and the statue exploded. Chunks of marble flew through the air. Sunshine whinnied and scrambled backwards but she couldn't move fast enough. A large stone wing came plummeting down from the sky towards Evie and Sunshine!

HAVE YOU READ?

Sophia and Rainbow

Scarlett and Blaze

Ava and Star

Isabel and Cloud

Layla and Dancer

Olivia and Snowflake

Rosa and Crystal

Ariana and Whisper

Matilda and Pearl

Freya and Honey

Violet and Twinkle

Isla and Buttercup

Lily and Feather

Phoebe and Shimmer

Zara and Moonbeam

Aisha and Silver

Lyra and Misty

LOOK OUT FOR:

Ivy and Flame

Evie and Sunshine

JULIE
SYKES

illustrated by
LUCY
TRUMAN

nosy
crow

For Nusaibah and Lauryn, who are super writers and know the magic of books.

First published in the UK in 2021 by Nosy Crow Ltd
The Crow's Nest, 14 Baden Place
Crosby Row, London, SE1 1YW

www.nosycrow.com

ISBN: 978 1 78800 963 8

Printed and bound in Great Britain by Clays Ltd, Elcograf S.p.A.

Papers used by Nosy Crow are made from
wood grown in sustainable forests.

1 3 5 7 9 10 8 6 4 2

CHAPTER ONE

"That was yummy," Evie said as she licked crumbs of chocolate cake from her fingers. The girls from Ruby dormitory were having a picnic in a corner of the walled orchard while their unicorns grazed on the lush grass. It was late spring, the apple trees were covered with white blossom and the bright sunlight, dappling through the branches, warmed Evie's face.

"OK," said Lyra, packing away the picnic things and double-checking that no one else was in sight. "Now for the important business that we came here to discuss."

"To solve the riddle on the treasure map!" said Sienna eagerly. She poked Ivy, who was lying on her back with her eyes shut. "Ivy, wake up!"

Ivy wriggled away. "I am awake. Have you got the map, Lyra?" She turned herself on to her tummy.

Evie and Sunshine

Lyra carefully pulled two yellowed squares of paper from her pocket. They crackled as she unfolded them and smoothed them out, placing them side by side on the picnic rug. Each one was part of a map that had been cut into four pieces. These two each had a small picture of a crying unicorn in their outside corners. Together they made up the top half of the map. They formed a picture of Unicorn Academy and, further down, part of a maze with half of a big X in the centre. The girls didn't know what the treasure in the maze was but they were determined to find out!

They had discovered the first piece hidden in a secret room above their dorm and Topaz dorm. A riddle on the back had led them to the second piece, which they had found behind an underground waterfall in the school grounds. They hoped that the riddle written on it would direct them to the third piece.

"This riddle is really annoying!" said Lyra. "What does it even mean?"

Evie pushed her wavy brown hair behind her ears. She had already memorised the riddle and recited it for the others:

"In a new folly that phantoms keep safe
There's a space you can enter and leave with no trace.
A cold place to rest hides the circular key,
Press once and enter the d-da-dark cavity."

As Evie stumbled over the last few words, she blushed. Sometimes her mouth just couldn't seem to keep up with her brain and her words came out muddled. Luckily her friends never mentioned it, but she hated when it happened. Similarly, when she was moving fast or playing sport, she often tripped over. But Evie didn't mind about not being great at sport – she preferred reading and wanted to be a scientist when she was older.

"I don't understand the first line," said Sienna.

"Phantoms are ghosts. But how can ghosts keep anywhere safe?"

"And what's 'a new folly'?" asked Ivy.

"'Folly' means foolish," said Evie shyly.

"A new foolish that ghosts keep safe?" said Lyra. "That doesn't make any sense." She rubbed her forehead in frustration.

The word *folly* was bothering Evie too. She'd heard it before and thought it had another meaning but she couldn't remember what.

"A cavity's a hole," said Sienna. "Could the dark cavity be the secret room where we found the first part of the map? You have to press a hidden circular button to open it up." Her eyes lit up. "Yes, maybe that's it!"

"But the secret room isn't dark," Lyra argued. "It has a window and it's not really a cavity."

Evie reached for the map but, as she did so, her arm knocked against her water bottle. She hadn't screwed the top on properly and water splashed out. She tried to grab it but her fingers fumbled and instead she sent it rolling towards the precious paper.

"No!" shrieked Sienna.

Luckily Lyra swept up the pieces of map before the water could reach them.

"I'm sorry!" cried Evie, jumping to her feet as Ivy pulled some tissues out of her pocket and started to mop up the water.

"What's going on?" Sunshine, Evie's elegant unicorn, came trotting over with the other unicorns – Misty, Flame and Sparkle.

"Just Evie being a clumsy doughnut again," said Sienna, grinning. "Honestly, Evie, I think we should ban you from being around food or drink. You always spill something!"

Even though Sienna was only teasing, Evie felt awful. She tried to help by brushing the remaining liquid from the rug but, as she stepped back, she tripped over Lyra's bag and fell over.

"Oh, Evie!" groaned Sunshine. She was a very pretty unicorn with yellow, turquoise and deep-pink patterns on her white coat that matched her long mane and tail.

"Evie, please go and stand by Sunshine and we'll clear up," said Ivy.

Evie went over to Sunshine and stroked her mane to hide her blushes. She wondered if Sunshine wished she had been paired with a different student – someone who wasn't so embarrassing. Sunshine hated being the centre of attention almost as much as Evie did.

How will we ever bond and graduate if Sunshine is embarrassed by me? Evie thought anxiously. During their time at Unicorn Academy the students learned how to become guardians of Unicorn Island. They couldn't graduate until they had bonded with their unicorn and discovered their unicorn's magic power. Bonding was the highest form of friendship and Evie would know when it happened because a lock of her hair would turn the same colour as Sunshine's mane.

Lyra and Misty were the only ones in Ruby dorm to have bonded so far – Lyra now had a purple, yellow and green streak in her hair to prove it. Misty was also the only unicorn in Ruby dorm to have found her magic. She could form protective bubbles around people in danger. Evie couldn't wait to discover what Sunshine's magic was!

"I vote we go and explore the hidden room again," said Sienna as Lyra and Ivy packed the rug and water bottles away. "But for now let's make the most of the sun and have an obstacle race. I bet there's some stuff in that shed we could use!"

Sienna ran to a nearby garden shed and began to pull things out. The others went to help but Sunshine stopped Evie.

"Let's just watch," she said.

Evie guessed Sunshine was worried that she would embarrass her if they tried to take part. "OK," she said with a sigh.

The others came back laden with buckets, beanpoles, plant pots, hoops and beanbags. Sienna instructed everyone where to put everything, and when the course was set up she shinned up an apple tree with a beanbag and balanced it on a branch.

"Listen up!" she said, sliding easily back down the trunk. "This is the course. First you gallop to the line of poles. You weave through them then race to the upturned bucket where you have to reach down and pick up a plant pot. Next, ride to the pole near the apple tree, put the pot on top then climb the apple tree to get the beanbag. Once you're back on your unicorn it's a race to the end, jumping over the fallen log and throwing the beanbag through this hoop as you cross the finishing line. Fastest time wins. Evie and Sunshine, you're up first."

Evie shook her head. "I'll just keep the times for everyone."

"Oh no, you've got to join in. We can all take turns at timing," said Sienna.

"Yes, please take part," said Ivy.

"Pleeeease, Evie!" begged Lyra. "It'll be more fun if we all do it."

Evie hated everyone focusing on her. "OK," she said, giving in, even though she could feel a knot of anxiety tightening in her chest. She saw Sunshine give her an alarmed look.

"Evie, I don't think this is a good idea," said Sunshine in a low voice as Evie got on to her back.

Evie swallowed. "I promise I'll try not to embarrass you," she murmured.

"It's not that. It's—"

"Come on, they're waiting for us to start," interrupted Evie.

Lyra had the stopwatch. "Three, two, one, go!" she shouted.

Sunshine reluctantly set off. Evie gripped her mane as they cantered to the poles. Sunshine weaved gracefully between them and Evie could hear the others cheering her on.

So far so good, she thought as Sunshine galloped on to the bucket and pole by the apple tree. Leaning down, she picked up the plant pot from the upturned bucket. *Don't drop it, don't drop it*, she told herself. To her relief Sunshine stood absolutely still while she slipped it on top of the pole. *Phew! Now for the tree!*

"Please be *very* careful," Sunshine begged her as Evie dismounted and ran over to it, skirting carefully round daffodils at the base of the trunk. Gritting her teeth, Evie pulled herself up until she reached the branch where the beanbag was balanced. Keeping one arm wrapped round the tree trunk, Evie stretched out to retrieve it.

Beneath her, Sunshine pawed at the ground anxiously. "Be careful, Evie!" she whinnied.

With a shriek, Evie overbalanced and hung underneath the branch, clinging on desperately with her hands and feet. She heard a faint popping noise and suddenly the tree shook violently as if it had just been hit. Evie gasped as her grip on the trunk loosened and she fell…

CHAPTER TWO

"Evie!" her friends yelled.

Sunshine whinnied and leapt forward to try to catch her but Misty was already stamping her hoof and using her magic. A large shimmering bubble formed round Evie and carried her gently to the ground where it came to a stop before popping. Evie sat on the grass, her heart pounding. If Misty hadn't used her magic, she could have been badly hurt.

"Are you OK?" Lyra, Ivy and Sienna demanded, galloping over on their unicorns.

"I'm fine!" said Evie, knowing her face was as

red as a tomato. She looked at the daffodils she had crushed when she landed. "I don't know what happened." She was sure she'd felt the tree shake when she'd been hanging on but maybe she'd imagined it. She'd probably just been dizzy because she'd been upside down. "Thanks, Misty."

"No problem," said Misty.

Sunshine seemed scared and embarrassed as she nuzzled her. "I'm really glad you're not hurt."

Lyra helped pull Evie to her feet. "Do you want to finish the course?" she asked.

Evie shook her head. "I think I'll head indoors," she said, pulling a twig from her hair.

"I'll come with you," Ivy offered.

"It's OK. I'll be fine." Evie's eyes smarted. Why couldn't she just be normal like everyone else? Her foot throbbed as she hobbled back to Sunshine. In silence they walked to the stables.

When they were back, Sunshine finally spoke.

"Next time there's an obstacle race or something like that I think we should just watch, Evie."

"OK," Evie muttered. She certainly didn't want to embarrass Sunshine any further.

After topping up Sunshine's hay net and fluffing up her straw bed, Evie left the stables. As she walked towards the school buildings, she felt her unhappiness lift. It was hard to be miserable when Unicorn Academy was so beautiful. The gardens were bursting with spring flowers and the glass and marble towers of the school sparkled against the clear blue sky. Evie's chest filled with pride. *I might not be good at sport but I'm a good student and I'm great at science and maths,* she reminded herself as she went inside. *There's no reason I can't be an excellent guardian of Unicorn Island.*

Sam, one of the boys from Topaz dorm, was coming along the corridor pulling a suitcase on wheels. A lady with a dark shoulder-length bob and lots of jewellery was walking beside him pulling a much larger case. Evie recognised her as Dr Angelica Briar, Sam's aunt and a famous archaeologist. She'd visited the academy earlier in the year to give a talk on her work and afterwards the Ruby girls had shown her the first part of the map they had found. Dr Briar had told them it was about a hundred years old but that it wasn't worth anything.

Sam whispered something to his aunt and then greeted Evie. "Hi there!"

"Hi, Sam," Evie said. "Hello, Dr Briar."

Dr Briar smiled warmly. "Evie, isn't it? You were one of the girls who found that old piece of paper, weren't you?"

Evie was thrilled that Dr Briar had remembered her. "Yes, that's right."

"Aunt Angelica is staying for a few weeks to help document the paintings and artefacts in the school," said Sam proudly.

"So, have you and your friends found any other bits of old paper that you want me to take a look at?" Dr Briar's eyes twinkled merrily.

Evie only just stopped herself from saying that they had found a second piece. She'd like to have told Dr Briar, but Lyra had made them promise to keep the map secret.

"Well?" pressed Dr Briar, her eyes curious.

"No." A blush crept up Evie's cheeks as she lied. To hide her discomfort she blurted out a question. "Dr Briar, do you know what 'folly' means?" She'd been pondering that ever since she'd been in the orchard.

"Why, yes I do," said Dr Briar. "It means foolish, but it's also the name given to a structure that's built for fun and which has no practical purpose. Many years ago rich people liked to build follies in the grounds of their houses. They could be towers or even miniature castles."

Of course! Evie suddenly remembered reading about a secret folly in a book. Her eyes widened. Maybe the *new folly* in the riddle was a building – a place that had recently been built when the map was drawn.

"Why do you ask?" Dr Briar asked, studying her.

"Oh, n-no reason," Evie stammered. "I just heard the word somewhere and didn't know what it meant." Evie felt uncomfortable under Dr Briar's scrutiny. "Right, well, I'd better go," she gabbled. "Nice to see you, Dr Briar. Bye, Sam!"

She didn't stop until she was back in Ruby dorm at the top of the north tower. She sank down on her bed, impatient for the others to come back so that she could tell them what she'd found out!

CHAPTER THREE

A little while later, Lyra and Sienna came bounding up the stairs with Ivy following more slowly.

"I won!" Sienna announced gleefully. "Ivy couldn't get the beanbag through the hoop and Lyra and Misty knocked a pole over."

Ivy flopped down on her bed. "I'm exhausted!"

"Is your foot OK?" Lyra asked Evie. "You looked like you were limping earlier."

Evie could hardly contain her excitement. "It's fine now. But I've got something to tell you all! I saw Dr Briar earlier and—"

"Dr Briar!" Lyra broke in. "Why's she back here? I know she's Sam's aunt but there's something about her that I don't trust."

"I know what you mean," Sienna added. "Remember when we showed her the first piece of the map and she looked like she wasn't going to give it back?"

"Yes, and—"

"Shush, you two!" interrupted Ivy. "Evie said she's got something to tell us. Go on, Evie."

Evie gave Ivy a grateful look. It was sometimes hard to get a word in edgeways when Sienna and Lyra got talking. She took a breath. "Dr Briar is here to document the paintings and stuff. I asked her if she knew what a folly was and she told me it's a building like a tower, often built in the grounds of a big house, that's just for fun."

"So there could be a folly here in the academy grounds?" said Lyra, her green eyes lighting up.

Evie nodded. "Or the riddle could mean elsewhere on the island."

"A folly guarded by ghosts," breathed Sienna.

They all looked at each other in excitement.

"This might be what we need to solve the riddle!" said Lyra. "You're a star, Evie!"

"Yes, you're absolutely a-mazing!" declared Sienna.

Evie glowed in delight at the praise.

Sienna grabbed Lyra's shoulder. "We're going to find the treasure map," she chanted.

"We're going to find the treasure!" Lyra sang back.

The door, which the girls had left ajar, opened and Nawaz, Archie and Reuben from Topaz dorm looked in.

"What are you lot shouting about?" asked Nawaz.

"Nothing!" Lyra said hastily.

Sam appeared behind the other boys. "What's going on?"

"The girls have gone loopy," said Reuben. "They were shouting about finding treasure."

Sam's face stiffened. "Treasure?"

"Lyra and Sienna were just messing around," said Ivy hastily.

"Hey, we were hoping to catch you," said Sienna. "We wanted to challenge you to a crossnet match tomorrow."

Evie smiled to herself – Sienna was so quick at making things up. It was the first she'd heard about a crossnet match.

"Ruby versus Topaz," added Lyra.

"Cool," said Archie.

They discussed the details and agreed to meet

at ten the next morning at the crossnet pitch. But as the boys left, Evie saw Sam give the girls an intent look very much like the look Dr Briar had given her in the corridor earlier.

"Whoops, that was close!" whispered Sienna, as Lyra shut the door.

Lyra pulled a face. "I can't believe we were stupid enough to shout about treasure. Did you see the way Sam was looking at us as he left? I hope he doesn't suspect anything. Remember when someone ransacked our dorm just after we found the first piece? We thought it was a prank but what if Dr Briar was lying when she said that the map wasn't valuable? What if she or Sam searched our dorm trying to find it?" She patted her pockets. "From now on these are never leaving my sight – we're not letting anyone else find the treasure!"

Evie couldn't sleep that night for thinking about the crossnet match. Crossnet was played with teams of two or four, and the idea was to ride up and down the pitch throwing the ball using sticks with nets on the end; goals were scored when the ball was put through the opposing team's hoop. Evie always ended up dropping the ball. It was fine playing with her friends, who never seemed to care, but it would be really embarrassing to mess up in front of Topaz dorm.

She got up at sunrise and went to the window. She could see right across the grounds. Beyond Lake Sparkle were the meadows, and past them were the woods where they'd found the cave that had led them to the underground river. On the other side of the woods was a smaller copse. One tree in the middle looked taller than the rest. Evie blinked. Was it a tree, or could it be the top of a tower? It was hard to tell. She glanced round at her sleeping

friends. Should she mention it to them? But if she did, Lyra would want to go there, and if Evie was wrong and it was just a tall tree, she'd feel really stupid. *Maybe I should do some research first,* she thought. *I could go to the library instead of playing crossnet.*

By the time the rest of Ruby dorm woke up Evie had come to a decision.

"I'm not going to play in the crossnet match," she told them. "I'm going to the library instead to see if I can find out if there are any follies in the school grounds."

"But if you don't play, we won't be able to have teams of four," said Sienna.

"You can play in pairs and add the points up over several rounds," Evie pointed out. "Or play in teams of three. That way one person from each dorm can act as a referee."

Lyra frowned. "This isn't because of what

28

happened in the obstacle race yesterday, is it?"

Evie rubbed her nose. "It is, kind of." *And it'll make Sunshine happier if I don't play and embarrass her,* she added to herself.

Ivy put her arm though Evie's. "We'd rather lose and have you as part of the team than win without you."

"Absolutely," said Lyra.

Evie saw Sienna hesitate, but then she nodded. "Of course we'd rather you played," she said.

Evie knew Sienna was being kind – she hated losing any competition – but she was grateful Sienna cared about her feelings enough to lie. "I really do want to do some research. You play without me."

Although Lyra and Ivy continued trying to change her mind, Evie stood her ground. When the others went to get their unicorns ready, she went with them to explain to Sunshine that she wasn't joining in with the match.

"Good. I think it's for the best," Sunshine said, looking relieved.

Evie felt a flicker of unhappiness. A small part of her had hoped that Sunshine would say that it didn't matter if she messed up, and reassure her that her friends meant it when they said they would rather she joined in. She sighed. "I guess so."

"You do *want* to miss the match, don't you, Evie?" said Sunshine, giving her a concerned look.

"Yes … No … I mean, I know it's for the best," said Evie. She hurried to the door and saw that Sunshine was watching her rather anxiously. "I'll get you some sky berries and then I'm going to the library."

Evie was coming back from the storeroom with a bucket of sky berries – the unicorns'

favourite food – when there was a loud bang from Sunshine's stable. Evie ran to the door.

Sunshine stood in the entrance. She was covered in bits of hay. It hung from her nose like a droopy moustache and stuck to her legs, making her look like a shaggy pony. A giggle rose in Evie's throat but Sunshine looked so shocked that she bit it back. "What's going on?"

"Um … I stamped my hoof and my-my hay net burst," stammered Sunshine.

Evie squeezed past her, her eyes widening as she took in the mess. "Are you sure you're OK? How did it happen?"

"It must have been the way you tied it up. It fell down and exploded," said Sunshine.

Evie felt shame rush through her. She *had* filled it very full but she thought she'd tied it up properly. "Oh, gosh. I'm so sorry! I'll refill it and sweep up."

"Don't worry. I can eat the hay from the floor," said Sunshine. "Just go!" she added quickly. "Please, Evie!"

Evie swallowed. "OK, well, see you later then." Feeling unhappy, she headed back to school. Unicorns and their partners were supposed to want to be together. If Sunshine wouldn't even let her clear up her stable, she must really be wishing that she'd been paired with someone else!

Evie went straight to the library and found a box of old maps in the reference section. She took one of the school grounds and carefully spread it out on a nearby table. The map smelled musty and the ink was beginning to fade. Evie pored over it. On the western side of the woods she saw the cave that had led to the underground river. Beyond that there was a smaller copse. The middle was marked with a triangle. She squinted at the old-fashioned writing next to it and read *folly*. Excitement leapt through her.

"Do you need any help?" Ms Tansy, the librarian, said, coming over and making Evie jump.

Evie looked up eagerly. "Do you know anything about this folly?"

Ms Tansy peered at the map through her yellow flower-shaped glasses. "I don't, but there's a book about follies of the island. It might be mentioned in there." She hurried off and returned with a thick book open in her hands. "Here you go," she said. *"The folly at the academy, built to look like an ancient tower, was constructed about a hundred years ago in the middle of Spiny Copse."*

A hundred years ago. Evie's brain whirred. Dr Briar had told them she thought the first piece of the map was about a hundred years old. Was that just coincidence or could this be the new folly mentioned in the clue, a folly built at the same time the map was made?

"Apparently there were all sorts of stories about it being haunted. After several students claimed they saw and heard ghosts near it, it was abandoned. There's a picture here – of the tower not the ghosts!" Ms Tansy chuckled.

Evie stared at the black-and-white photo that showed a round stone building topped with a cone-shaped turret. An idea grew in her mind as she recalled a line from the riddle: *In a new folly that phantoms keep safe.* Was the tower really haunted or had someone started that rumour to keep people away after hiding part of the treasure map there?

Evie asked if she could borrow the book and Ms Tansy carried it over to her desk and checked it out. As she passed it back to Evie, Dr Briar arrived.

"Hello, Evie."

"Hello," said Evie. Her fingers fumbled with the book and it thudded to the floor.

"Allow me." Dr Briar picked the book up and glanced at the title. "Follies," she said, raising her eyebrows. "You were asking me about follies yesterday, weren't you?"

Evie nodded.

"Do you have a particular interest in them?" Dr Briar asked.

"Evie is one of our keenest readers," said Ms Tansy warmly. "She's interested in everything. We were just talking about the folly in the school grounds. Maybe you know something about it, Dr Briar? Apparently it's haunted!"

Dr Briar smiled. "Apparently so, if you believe in ghosts. Although there have been many sightings so maybe there is truth in the stories after all!" She turned to Evie. "Why are you so interested in the school folly? That wasn't where you and your friends found that old piece of paper you showed me, was it?"

"No," said Evie, glad to be telling the truth. "It wasn't."

"I'd be very careful if you're planning an excursion there," said Dr Briar, studying her closely. "The building is very old and it may be dangerous."

Evie felt a blush rise in her cheeks. "Thanks!"

Dr Briar studied her as if she was an artefact under a microscope.

Evie got redder and redder.

Ms Tansy looked from one to the other, a puzzled frown forming between her eyes. "Well, run along now, Evie dear," she said brightly, breaking the silence.

Dr Briar handed Evie the book. "Yes, off you go," she said.

Evie hurried out of the library in relief. But as she reached the door she glanced back and saw Dr Briar watching her leave.

CHAPTER FOUR

Evie settled down in the dorm and read, her eyes quickly skimming over the words. The folly in the grounds had been built a hundred years ago by a headteacher called Ms Evergreen. According to the book, Ms Evergreen had been a fascinating woman, intrepid and brave and a passionate guardian of the island. Before becoming headteacher she had been an archaeologist and had spent many years searching for a precious jewel known as the Unicorn's Diamond.

"The Unicorn's Diamond," Evie whispered aloud, feeling a shiver of excitement. The diamond was legendary for both its beauty and its power.

Just then her friends came up the stairs, chattering loudly.

Sienna threw the door open. "We won. We beat the boys five matches to three."

"It was fun and when we got back to the stables, there was an explosion!" added Lyra. "One of the automated trolleys was trundling along with a bucket full of sky berries. It was just passing Sunshine's stable when there was a loud bang. The berries exploded and went everywhere."

"Really?" Evie's eyes widened. "Was anyone hurt?"

Ivy grinned. "No, but there was a huge mess. We had to wash Sunshine's mane. It turned blue with sky berry juice. "

"Is she OK?"

"She's fine," said Ivy, putting a reassuring

arm round Evie. "Ms Tulip thought the berries may have exploded because they were from last season and they'd been left in a warm cupboard. Sunshine seemed a bit shocked at first but we cleaned her up and left her munching on a hay net. She said not to tell you but we thought you'd want to know."

Evie wondered why Sunshine hadn't wanted her to come and help but she pushed the thought away as she remembered her news. "You'll never guess what I've found out," she said.

They all sat on her bed while Evie explained what she'd discovered about the folly in the grounds.

"Ms Evergreen, who built it, was headteacher here a hundred years ago. She sounds awesome. She was previously an archaeologist and she'd spent years searching for the Unicorn's Diamond."

"The Unicorn's Diamond," said Lyra thoughtfully. "A beautiful diamond that grants the heart's desire of anyone who holds it. Isn't that just a legend?"

"This book says no one knows for sure," said Evie. She glanced at its pages. "The legend is that it was created in ancient times, formed from the tears of joy shed by Unicorn Island's original unicorn, Daybreak, on the birth of her first foal. The—"

"Daybreak?" interrupted Sienna. "Hang on! Isn't that the unicorn on the tapestry downstairs that hides the entrance to the secret room?"

"Yes, and we had to follow carvings of Daybreak to get to the second piece of the map," said Ivy.

Evie gasped loudly.

"What is it?" demanded Lyra.

"Have … have you got the – the map?" Evie asked, stumbling over her words in her excitement.

"Yes. Why?" Lyra pulled the pieces out of her pocket and smoothed them out.

"Look!" Evie's voice came out as a squeak as she stabbed her finger at the top corner of each piece. "There are pictures of Daybreak here too, in each corner. Could the map take you to—"

"The Unicorn's Diamond!" finished Lyra.

They all stared at each other.

"Do you really think this map could lead us to the diamond?" whispered Sienna.

"Yes! I do!" Evie picked up her book again and read a paragraph out. *"According to the legend, anyone who holds the diamond in their hand will be granted their heart's desire. For centuries people have sought the diamond in order to ask for their greatest wish. But the diamond, if it ever existed, has been so well hidden that so far no one has found it."* She looked up, her eyes shining. "But maybe Ms Evergreen did find it—"

Lyra broke in. "And hid it somewhere safe so that people couldn't get their hands on it. It would be awful if it was found by someone who wanted to make bad things happen."

Evie nodded. "But Ms Evergreen made a map so that it could be found again if it needed to be. She cut it into four and hid the pieces in the school grounds."

"And if we find the rest of the map, we'll find the diamond!" said Lyra, looking as if she was about to burst with excitement.

"We've got to find it," said Sienna.

Lyra jumped up. "Let's go and find the folly right now!"

"We can't," said Ivy. "It's lunchtime."

"After lunch then," said Lyra.

"No, Spiny Copse, where the folly is, is at the edge of the school grounds," said Evie. "We won't be able to get there and back before dark. We'll have to wait until Saturday – three days' time."

Sienna nodded. "We could tell Ms Rivers we want to look at the wildlife and ask if we can take a picnic with us, then we can have the whole day to explore the tower."

There was a faint noise outside their dorm door. Lyra hurried over and pulled the door open but there was no one there.

She shut it behind her again. "Phew! I thought

for a moment someone was listening to us. This must stay as our secret. We can't tell anyone about it. Promise?"

They all nodded. "Promise!"

CHAPTER
FIVE

At breakfast the following morning, Evie was astonished when Dr Briar beckoned her over to where she was sitting with Ms Nettles.

"Evie, I wonder if I could ask you for a favour." The jewelled rings on Dr Briar's fingers flashed as she patted a strand of her sleek dark hair into place. "The academy has many more works of art than I realised. Would you like to help me today?"

"Me?" Evie was confused. Had Dr Briar really meant to ask her or had she meant Lyra, who everyone knew wanted to be an archaeologist when she was older?

But no, Dr Briar was looking right at her and smiling encouragingly.

Evie's cheeks heated up. It was lovely – if slightly astonishing – to be singled out in such a way. "Yes, please," she said immediately.

"Perfect. Meet me in the hall at lunchtime and I'll show you what needs to be done."

Evie almost floated out of the dining room but Lyra frowned when Evie told them what the conversation had been about. "She asked you to help? Why? I mean, no offence, Evie, but you are quite accident-prone. And Sam knows how much I love archaeology. Surely he'd have suggested Dr Briar ask me not you." Her frown deepened. "Make sure you don't tell them anything about the map."

"Evie's not stupid; of course she won't say anything," said Ivy.

Evie was hurt that Lyra had felt a reminder was

needed and while the others got ready for their first lesson – science – she went to the stables to talk to Sunshine about it.

As she approached Sunshine's stall, Evie heard a bang and saw a pink spark shoot out of the doorway. Evie rushed forward, her heart in her mouth. "Sunshine!" she cried. "Was that you? Have you found your magic?"

Sunshine popped her head out of her stable.

"No!" she said quickly. "I haven't. Definitely not! Why are you here, Evie?"

Her voice was almost unfriendly. Evie stopped in her tracks. She thought she'd seen a spark of magic. "I … I just wanted to talk to you about something."

"Can't it wait?" said Sunshine. She didn't seem to want Evie to go into her stable.

"Yes, I guess," said Evie uncomfortably. Sunshine had never been so short with her before. "I'll … um … come back later."

"I'll see you at break then," said Sunshine.

Evie turned away. What was up with Sunshine? She was acting as though Evie had really upset her. Feeling bewildered, Evie headed back to school.

Evie didn't go and see Sunshine at break. She didn't want to risk her unicorn being unfriendly to her in front of everyone. At lunchtime she waited for Dr Briar in the hall. In the centre of the room was the magic map, which showed the whole of Unicorn Island. It could transport people and their unicorns anywhere on the island but there was a magical force field protecting it and students were only allowed to use it with a teacher's permission.

The walls of the hall were covered with enormous paintings of famous unicorns and previous headteachers. When Dr Briar arrived with Sam, she asked Sam and Evie to work their way round the room writing down the title and artist of each painting as well as making some brief notes.

Evie felt shy at first. Sam often acted in a superior way but now it was just the two of them he was much more friendly. He knew lots of interesting stories about the artists who had painted the pictures.

"How do you know so much?" she asked.

"My mum's an art historian," Sam replied. "She's taught me lots about art. I often spend time with Aunt Angelica in the holidays too." He nodded towards Dr Briar, who was studying a large pink vase in an alcove. "I've helped her on tons of digs." He smiled at Evie. "I don't know nearly as much as you do about science and maths though. You're really clever."

Evie felt a warm glow. "Thanks,' she muttered, thinking how much nicer Sam was when he was on his own.

Sam's aunt called him over and had a low conversation with him. When he returned, he looked slightly uncomfortable. "So," he said, "what have you and the rest of your dorm been getting up to? You always seem to be whispering about something. What's the big secret?"

Evie was surprised at the change of subject. "Nothing," she said, blushing. "There's no big secret at all. Who's this painting by?" she asked, moving on to a portrait of a previous headteacher.

"Finoula Sparrow," said Sam, following her. "Did you know there are supposed to be lots of secret passageways and hidden rooms in the academy? I'd love to find one, wouldn't you?" He looked at her intently.

"I guess," said Evie uneasily.

"But you haven't found any secret places yet?" pressed Sam.

"No, definitely not," said Evie quickly. She turned away. "I'm going to make some notes on the statues over there."

As she walked away from Sam, she glanced at Dr Briar and she saw her giving Sam a questioning look.

He shook his head. Evie frowned, suddenly certain that Dr Briar and Sam were up to something. Why had Dr Briar asked her to help and not Lyra? Did she think that Evie would tell her more about what they were up to?

Well, they can try all they like, but they're not going to get any information about the map from me, she thought determinedly.

She stopped by the statues and wrote down some notes. Her scalp prickled. She was sure Dr Briar and Sam were both still watching her. But why?

After lunch, in the geography and culture lesson, Ms Rivers announced that they were going on a statue hunt in the school grounds with their unicorns.

"I'll give you a list of artefacts to find," Ms Rivers told them. "Answer the questions about them and the first team to arrive back with the correct answers will win a prize."

"This is the best lesson ever!" said Sienna as they fetched their unicorns.

Sam and the boys from Topaz were ready first. "We are so going to win! Watch us and weep, Ruby dorm!" he cried, before galloping away with his friends.

"I don't know how you coped with having to spend all lunchtime with him," Sienna said to Evie, pulling a face.

"It was a bit weird," said Evie. She wondered whether to mention her suspicions about Sam and Dr Briar, but she didn't have any proof so she decided to keep quiet for now.

To Evie's relief Sunshine seemed back to her usual friendly self that afternoon. "This is fun!" she whinnied as they galloped towards the rose gardens with the others.

Evie and Sunshine

The girls visited the rose gardens, the safari trail, the play park, the vegetable garden and the lake, ticking nine of the ten items off their list. "We just need a winged unicorn statue now," said Lyra.

"There's one in the orchard," said Evie.

As they approached the orchard, the boys appeared at a gallop from the direction of the play park. "Faster! They're going to the orchard too," Sienna shouted.

Ruby dorm raced into the orchard with the Topaz boys right behind them. The rearing unicorn with wings was on a plinth by a pear tree. Sunshine reached the statue first. She halted abruptly in front of it, making Evie slip sideways on her back. "Are you OK, Evie?" Sunshine said, anxiously stamping her feet.

"Yes, yes, I'm—"

But Evie broke off as there was a flash of pink and the statue exploded.

Evie and Sunshine

Chunks of marble flew through the air. Sunshine whinnied and scrambled backwards but she couldn't move fast enough. A large stone wing came plummeting down from the sky towards them!

CHAPTER SIX

The wing hurtled towards Evie and Sunshine. Evie was sure it was going to hit them but at the very last moment time seemed to pause. The wing froze in the air above their heads. Sunshine reared backwards and then time restarted.

Whumph! The marble wing thumped into the ground exactly where Evie and Sunshine had been a few seconds ago.

"Evie! Sunshine! Are you OK?' cried Lyra.

"What happened?" gasped Evie. "I thought it was going to hit us but it just stopped in mid-air!"

"It was Flash!" Sam burst out, jumping off and

hugging his unicorn. "I saw sparks fly from his hooves and I smelled burnt sugar. He must have got his magic – pausing magic! It will mean he can make things stop for a few seconds."

"Oh, wow!" said Evie. "That's awesome magic. You saved our lives, Flash. Thank you so much. You're amazing!"

Flash, a tall unicorn with a silver and green mane, looked very proud as everyone crowded round, congratulating him and Sam.

"Now you've found your magic, we just need to bond and then we'll be able to graduate at the end of the year," said a beaming Sam, giving Flash another hug.

"Something we're forgetting to ask," said Lyra, frowning as she looked at the chunks of marble lying on the grass all around them, "is why the statue exploded in the first place."

"You didn't bump into it, did you?" Sienna asked Evie.

"No!" Evie said indignantly.

"It's really weird," said Lyra, riding round the plinth. "Statues shouldn't just explode for no reason. I guess we'd better tell Ms Rivers."

"We'll tell her," said Sam. "We're the fastest dorm. Come on, guys!" He vaulted back on to Flash and he and the other boys raced off.

Sienna scowled. "Sam can be so annoying."

"He did save me and Sunshine though," said

Evie. "I wonder why that statue exploded…"

"Evie, can we go back to the stables now?" Sunshine said. "I'm feeling a bit shaky."

"Of course," said Evie, patting her. "She turned back to the others. "You know, there have been quite a few explosions recently."

"What do you mean?" asked Ivy.

"Well, the sky berries exploded when you were at the stables and Sunshine's hay net burst the day before. I thought it was my fault, that I had stuffed it too full and hadn't tied it up properly but—"

"Evie, I really do want to go back," interrupted Sunshine loudly. "I'm not feeling well."

"OK," said Evie. "I'd better go," she told the others.

"We'll come with you," said Lyra, riding up alongside them. "The boys have won the treasure hunt now anyway. So you think someone might be making things explode around us on purpose?"

"Maybe it's someone who knows we've found the part of the map," said Sienna. "And they want to scare us."

"Or injure us," said Ivy with a shiver.

"But the only people who know we have a piece of the map are Dr Briar and Sam," said Evie.

Lyra looked thoughtful. "The statue exploded just as Sam reached it and he was there that day in the stables when the sky berries exploded." Her mouth tightened. "I bet Dr Briar is getting him to scare us because she knows we've found part of the map and wants it for herself. I knew she was interested in it, even though she pretended it was worthless!"

"But Sam can't be making things explode. Flash has pausing magic, not exploding magic," Evie pointed out.

"True, but maybe there's a spell or potion that can cause explosions," said Lyra. "Well, Sam and

Dr Briar had better watch out. They're not going to stop us finding the next part of the map. No way! We're going to search the folly on Saturday and then the third piece will be ours!"

On Saturday the girls woke early. They had permission from Ms Rivers to go on a picnic ride, so they went to the dining room to collect their packed lunches. On the table next to their lunches there was also a packed lunch with Dr Briar's name on it.

Lyra frowned. "Why does Dr Briar need a packed lunch?"

"Who cares," said Sienna. "Let's get going."

They grabbed some fresh croissants to eat on the way and set off.

It was another gorgeous day. Sparkle Lake glittered in the bright sunshine and the air was full of birdsong. The unicorns cantered through the meadows and then paused at the stream to give the unicorns a drink. They rode on through the beautiful academy grounds, but as they got closer to Spiny Copse the birds fell quiet and a shadow seemed to cross the sun. The tall, forbidding trees clustered closely together as if they wanted to keep people out. Creepers wound round their trunks and the shadows between them were dark and dense. The girls halted at the start of the path, no one wanting to be the first to enter.

Ivy shivered. "What if the folly really is haunted?"

"It's not," said Lyra. "There are no such things as ghosts."

"You hope!" Sienna said.

Evie thought back to what Ms Tansy had said about some students thinking they'd seen ghosts near the folly and hoped it was a rumour encouraged by Ms Evergreen to keep people away!

Lyra rode into the trees and Sienna and Ivy followed. To Evie's surprise Sunshine hung back.

"Come on," she said. "We don't want to get left behind."

Sunshine cantered after the others but Evie could feel her trembling. She frowned. Sunshine wasn't usually timid when it came to adventures, so what was bothering her?

The path was narrow and gloomy, the trees

blocking out the light. The wood was strangely silent and the air felt like icy fingers stroking their faces. As the unicorns pushed their way along the overgrown path the branches tugged at their legs and tails and the shadows deepened.

"I really don't like it here,' said Ivy nervously.

"Neither do I," said Sunshine to Evie. "It's so dark."

An eerie "WHOOOO-OOOO" rang through the air and a pale shape glimmered for a moment high in the trees before disappearing.

Ivy shrieked and Evie grabbed a handful of mane as Sunshine shied violently. Sienna gasped. "Was that a ghost?"

"It can't have been," said Lyra. She stroked Misty, who was trembling. "Ghosts aren't real."

"I really don't like this, Evie," said Sunshine, her voice quivering.

Evie took a deep breath to calm her racing heart. "Don't worry, I'm sure we'll be OK," she reassured her. "Lyra's right: ghosts aren't real."

"It's not the ghosts; it's the…" Sunshine's voice trailed off. "It doesn't matter," she muttered.

"We've got to keep going," said Lyra, urging Misty forward. "Look, there's something over there, through the trees!"

Evie caught a glimpse of golden stone in the distance. "I bet it's the folly. Come on, Sunshine, we're almost there!"

They all rode on. As the track widened out, Evie saw a tall tower made of yellow stone in a clearing ahead. Its crumbling walls looked like they were being held together by the thick swaths of dark-green ivy that covered them. There was an old wooden door with a stone bench outside it. Excitement bubbled up inside Evie, squashing her fears. This could be it! They 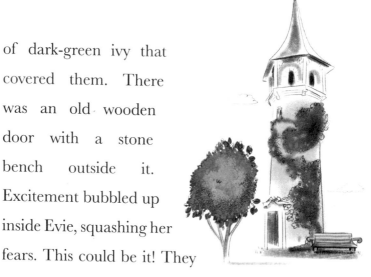 could be about to find the third piece of the map!

Sunshine halted by the bench. "Oh, wow," breathed Evie, dismounting and walking towards the tower.

"This is so exciting!" said Lyra, as Misty stopped beside Sunshine and she jumped off too. "I hope we find the—"

Then she gasped as the door opened and Dr Briar walked out!

CHAPTER SEVEN

"Hello, girls." Dr Briar smiled brightly as a tall, slim unicorn came out of the tower beside her. "Ms Nettles mentioned you were going out for a picnic ride today. I hope you weren't planning on exploring this folly?"

The Ruby girls gaped at her. Even Lyra seemed lost for words.

Dr Briar sighed. "It is a very interesting building but I'm afraid that you can't come inside. My research suggests that a previous headteacher may have hidden a special artefact here. Ms Nettles has given me permission to conduct a search. The tower and these woods are now out of bounds to all students until I have completed my work. I'm sure you understand." She continued to smile but Evie saw a distinct hint of triumph in her eyes.

"How did you get here so fast?" said Lyra, finding her voice at last. "You were still at school when we left."

"Solomon and I used the magic map," said Dr Briar, patting her unicorn. "It makes travelling between here and the school so much easier, but, of course, students aren't allowed to use it. Now, off you go. I'm sure you can find another place to have your little –" she paused – "*picnic*."

Evie couldn't bear the thought of Dr Briar finding the next clue before them, but there was absolutely nothing they could do about it. She walked heavily over to Sunshine but as she reached her, her foot snagged on a tree root, sending her sprawling.

"Are you OK?" Ivy called.

"I'm fine." Evie put her hand on the stone bench to pull herself up but as she did so her eyes fell on a small round indentation under one arm of the bench. The circle contained a tiny picture of a crying unicorn. Evie gave a strangled gasp. It looked exactly like the button that opened the staircase to the hidden room where they had found the first part of the map.

A line from the clue jumped into her head: *A cold place to rest hides the circular key.* Could this be it – the way to find the third piece? After all, the bench was definitely a cold place to rest…

"Evie?" said Lyra in concern. "Are you hurt?"

"N-no," Evie stammered, getting to her feet.

She could feel Dr Briar watching them but didn't want to say anything in front of her. "I'm fine. Let's go." She got back on to Sunshine and the girls left.

"I can't believe Dr Briar is searching the folly!" Lyra hissed when they were out of earshot.

"It's so not fair!" said Sienna.

"Dr Briar's bound to find the next part of the map before us now," groaned Ivy.

"Maybe not," said Evie, her eyes shining.

They all looked at her. "What do you mean?" asked Lyra.

"I'll tell you when we're somewhere properly private," said Evie, glancing around at the trees. There was no knowing who or what was lurking in them. "Come on!"

Only when they reached a meadow far away from the copse did Evie ask Sunshine to stop. She slid off and the others joined her as she sat down on the grass. "I saw something," she said. Even though they were absolutely on their own, she kept her voice low as she told them about the button she'd spotted under the bench.

"Think of the other two bits of the map," Evie said eagerly. "They were really well hidden. There's no way Ms Evergreen would have just left the third piece lying around in the tower. She's bound to have put it in a good hiding place. I think the button is important. Remember the riddle. It says:

In a new folly that phantoms keep safe

There's a space you can enter and leave with no trace.

A cold place to rest hides the circular key,

Press once and enter the dark cavity."

She looked at her friends. "I think the button is the circular key, and the map's hiding place – *the dark cavity* – will be revealed if we press it!"

"I bet you're right!" Lyra cried.

"So Dr Briar won't find the map unless she finds that button," said Sienna, smiling. "But because she hasn't seen the second piece, she won't even know to look for it!"

"We can still beat her!" exclaimed Ivy.

"How are we going to get into the tower without her seeing?" asked Evie. She sighed. "I guess we just have to wait until she abandons her search."

Lyra grinned. "Or we go to the tower when she's not there – at night!"

"No way!" Ivy squeaked.

"I'm with Ivy. Those woods are scary enough in the day," agreed Sienna.

"You want to find the map, don't you?" Lyra said.

They nodded.

"Then stop worrying about ghosts and get ready for a midnight adventure!" she declared.

CHAPTER EIGHT

"I don't understand. Why is Dr Briar searching the folly?" said Sienna as they got into their beds that night. They had decided to get some sleep before setting off at midnight when everyone else in the school would be in bed. "I mean, how did she guess there's a piece of the map there?"

"I don't know," said Lyra, pulling her red-spotted duvet cover up to her chin. "You didn't say anything when you were helping her, did you, Evie?"

"Evie wouldn't," said Ivy loyally.

Evie felt uncomfortable. "I didn't say anything

but it might have been my fault that she guessed about the folly." Her friends looked at her as she confessed. "I bumped into Dr Briar that time I went to the library and she saw me taking out the book on follies. She must have decided that I was interested in the school folly. I'm really sorry I wasn't more careful." She glanced up, wondering if the others were going to be cross with her, but they all just shrugged.

"It's not your fault. There's no way you could have known Dr Briar was going to be in the library as well," said Ivy. "Or that she'd realise why you had a book on follies."

"And if you hadn't borrowed that book, we might never have known about the folly ourselves," Sienna pointed out.

"I'm glad you went to the library that day," said Lyra.

Evie felt a rush of relief.

"If it's anyone's fault, it's mine and Sienna's," Lyra went on. "We were the ones who were shouting about treasure. I bet Sam told Dr Briar about it and that made her suspicious. I reckon she was listening in when we were talking about going to the folly. Remember there was that noise outside our door? It could have been her."

"Or Sam," added Sienna.

"You've definitely not got anything to feel bad about, Evie," said Ivy, smiling at her. "If it hadn't been for you, we'd never have found the secret button at the folly."

"Or the one that opened the staircase to the hidden room," said Lyra.

"I only found those buttons by falling over," said Evie.

"It's a very special talent, Evie," Sienna said.

"I'd call it unique," Lyra joined in with a grin.

"Definitely!" chuckled Ivy.

Evie saw the warmth in her friends' eyes and the knot of anxiety in her chest loosened. For the first time she started to believe that the rest of her dorm really didn't care that she was always having accidents and that maybe they did like her just the way she was.

"You're so clever, Evie," Ivy said, yawning as she turned off the light. "We wouldn't know nearly as much as we do now if we didn't have you."

I wish Sunshine felt the same, Evie thought as she snuggled down in bed. Sunshine had been fine with her when they'd been riding out to the tower but she'd been quiet on the way home and when they got back she'd seemed keen for Evie to leave her. Evie remembered all the times in the last week when Sunshine had wanted her to go away. *I wish she liked me more,* she thought sadly, *but I bet she wishes she had another partner.*

She comforted herself by remembering what her friends had just said. *I love being in Ruby dorm*, thought Evie happily, and with a smile she fell asleep.

At midnight the girls got out of their beds, dressed and crept down the stairs. Evie was glad of her warm coat as she stepped outside. The night was chilly. Unseen creatures rustled and squeaked from the bushes and somewhere nearby, an owl hooted. Evie glanced back and saw a shadow move behind one of the upper windows where the staff bedrooms were. Her heart leapt into her throat. Was someone there, watching them? But no. When she looked again, the shadows behind the window were still.

"Come on!" Ivy grabbed her hand and they ran silently across the dew-soaked grass to the stables, Ivy's grip tightening on Evie's whenever

Evie's feet tripped on a tuft of grass.

Entering the stables, Evie's cheeks tingled with the sudden warmth. She went quickly to Sunshine's stall, treading softly so as not to disturb the other unicorns, snuffling and snoring in their sleep.

Sunshine was awake, her dark eyes full of anxiety.

"We're still going then?" she asked Evie.

"Yes." Evie sensed her unicorn's reluctance.

"Why? Don't you want to?"

Sunshine looked awkward. "I do. It's just…" She trailed off.

Evie braced herself, sure that Sunshine was worried she was going to embarrass them in some way tonight. "What is it, Sunshine? Please tell me what's bothering you."

Sunshine glanced at her through her eyelashes. "I'm … I'm scared of the dark, Evie!"

Evie blinked. Of all the things she had been expecting Sunshine to say, it wasn't that. Hiding her surprise, she stroked Sunshine's cheek. "Really? But why?"

"I always have been." Sunshine shuddered. "The copse was bad enough by day; it's going to be even more scary at night."

"But Lyra's got a torch, so we'll have light,' said Evie gently. "And we'll all be together. Nothing will happen to you." As she reassured her, she felt a rush of relief. So this was why Sunshine had been quiet on the way home. It wasn't because she had been worried about Evie embarrassing her; it was because she'd been feeling scared about going back in the dark. "I'm really glad you told me," she said softly as Sunshine nuzzled her hands.

"Thanks for not laughing at me, Evie," Sunshine said gratefully. "I didn't want to say anything because I was worried that you'd think I was stupid."

"I'd never think that," said Evie, stroking her.

Sunshine blew softly at Evie's face. "I'm really glad that you're my partner, Evie. Look, there's something I need to tell you—"

"Are you two ready?" interrupted Lyra, looking into Sunshine's stable. "We haven't got much time," she added.

Evie sent Sunshine an apologetic look. "Tell me later," she whispered.

They followed the others outside and, mounting their unicorns, they set off at a gallop.

When they reached Spiny Copse, they stopped. A bat swooped past chasing a moth as Lyra shone her powerful torch down the path.

Sienna gulped. "What if we see that ghost thing again?"

"It wasn't a ghost," said Lyra firmly.

"So what was it? It certainly sounded spooky. *Whooooo*," said Sienna, mimicking the sound.

"I don't know what it was, but I promise you it wasn't a ghost," said Lyra, and she rode Misty into the trees.

Evie felt Sunshine hesitate and stroked her neck. "Don't be scared," she whispered. "Just focus on the light of the torch."

Sunshine nuzzled her leg before trotting after the others. To Evie's relief they reached the clearing with no ghostly encounters.

When they got there, they saw that Dr Briar had secured the tower's wooden door with a sturdy new padlock.

"Hopefully we won't need to use the door," said Lyra. "Where's that button, Evie? Let's press it and see what happens."

Evie slipped off Sunshine and crouched by the bench. Her fingers found the round indentation underneath it. "Here goes!" She pushed it in.

There was a creaking, rumbling sound and part of the outer wall of the tower juddered slowly back.

"Oh, wow! There's a secret space between

the tower's inner and outer walls," said Lyra, jumping off Misty and going over.

"A cavity!" exclaimed Sienna. "Just like the riddle said."

The space inside was as black as ink. Evie felt very impressed as she peered inside. Ms Evergreen must have been a brilliant engineer to have constructed such a thing.

"I'm going in," said Lyra excitedly. They all followed – unicorns too. "Everyone look for the map!"

Evie's eyes followed the beam of the torch as Lyra shone it around. The cavity ran all round the outside of the tower. High above them was a window with no glass. It had a wide, thick window ledge and there was something bulky on it, but it was impossible to see what it was in the darkness. "Lyra, shine your torch up there," she said.

Lyra did so and Evie saw a large nest of twigs.

Four spectre owlets with fluffy grey baby feathers that glowed in the moonlight peered over the top, their large round eyes glowing in the torch beam.

Just then there was a hooting noise – "WHOOOO-OOOO" – and the mother owl flew in through the window, the feathers on her silvery wings shimmering. She landed on the nest and peered down curiously at the girls.

Evie burst out laughing. "I think we've just found our ghost!"

"It was a spectre owl!" said Ivy, her face a picture of relief. "They glow in the moonlight."

Sienna heaved a sigh. "Phew!"

"I wonder if Ms Evergreen encouraged spectre owls to nest here all those years ago," said Evie. "To make people think the folly was haunted."

Lyra swept her torch away from the nest so as not to disturb the owls any longer and they continued to explore round the wall.

They were about halfway round when Ivy cried out. "Stop, Lyra! There's an alcove here."

Lyra shone the torch up the wall, revealing a small space carved into the stone about two metres up. Lyra scrambled on to Misty and stood up on her back. She reached into the alcove and gasped. "There's something here! I can feel it!"

She pulled out some folded paper. Her eyes were huge in the torchlight as she sat down on Misty's back and held it out for everyone to see. It was old and yellow with spots of brown. Lyra's breath caught in her throat as she opened it up. "It's the third piece of the map!"

She turned it over and they saw four lines of writing on the back.

"Another clue!" Evie exclaimed.

"If we solve it, we'll get the final part!" said Ivy in excitement.

"And then we can find the Unicorn's Diamond!"

cried Sienna.

A grating noise echoed round the tower wall. Lyra's head snapped up. "What's that?"

The walls were moving, and groaned as they scraped across the ground to close up the gap.

"The entrance is shutting again! Move it, everyone!" Lyra yelled.

They turned and raced back to where they had come in but they were too late. With a deafening crash the two walls met and the entrance disappeared. Evie's heart pounded against her ribs. They were trapped!

CHAPTER NINE

"What happened?" cried Sienna, banging on the crack between the walls where the entrance had been.

"Why did the walls just shut like that?" said Ivy, her eyes scared.

"Listen!" Lyra motioned for everyone to stop talking.

Muffled voices came from the other side of the tower's walls. It sounded like two people arguing.

"There's someone out there," said Sienna, frowning.

"Let us out!" shouted Lyra, thumping on the stone. The others joined in.

A sheet of paper suddenly slid through the crack between the two walls. Evie grabbed it. The paper was folded in half. Her fingers shook as she opened it and read aloud:

"HAND OVER THE MAP PIECES. IN RETURN YOU WILL BE SET FREE. NO MAP, NO ESCAPE."

The girls stared at each other.

"Someone's locked us in here on purpose!" said Ivy.

"Dr Briar, it has to be," said Lyra grimly.

"She can't have the map – not when we're so close to finding the treasure," said Sienna.

Evie bit her lip. "We don't have a choice. Unless we hand it over, we could be trapped here forever."

Lyra's torch flickered. "The batteries are running out." She shook the torch in alarm.

"You mean we're going to be trapped in the dark?" Sunshine burst out.

"It's OK, Sunshine," said Evie soothingly. "Just stay calm."

"I can't!" Sunshine's voice rose in panic as the torch beam flickered again. "No!" she whinnied, stamping her front hooves. Sparks flew up and hit the wall. The stone shattered, and the girls shrieked as their unicorns dodged the flying shards.

Evie and Sunshine

Lyra gasped. "What just happened?"

"It was Sunshine!" Ivy said, her eyes wide.

"Sunshine, you've just found your magic!" exclaimed Evie. "You've got exploding magic!"

To her surprise Sunshine hung her head. "Actually I, um … I haven't just found it. I discovered it a few days ago. All the explosions that have been happening – they're all my fault. Whenever I feel anxious and stamp my hooves, things just explode around me."

Evie stared at her. "Why didn't you tell me?"

Sunshine swallowed. "I didn't think you'd be very happy about me having exploding magic."

"Oh, Sunshine," said Evie, hugging her. "Of course I'm happy. Exploding magic is cool." A thought struck her. "Is this why you've been asking me to leave you alone all week? You didn't want me to find out?"

Sunshine nodded. "I can't control it and I

thought you'd find that really embarrassing. It's awful. I almost killed us when the unicorn statue exploded."

"So that was you, not Dr Briar or Sam?" Sienna said.

"Yes," muttered Sunshine

"You should have told me. I could have helped you," said Evie. She hugged her unicorn tightly. "I thought that you wanted a different partner. I'm so embarrassing. It's true," she added when Sunshine started to shake her head. "I'm always having accidents. I know that's why you try to stop me from doing things."

"It's not that," said Sunshine in surprise. "I only want to stop you from getting hurt." She nuzzled Evie. "But what about you? Are you OK about me having exploding magic? You don't like being the centre of attention and my magic is pretty hard to ignore."

Evie and Sunshine

Evie grinned. "I'm accident-prone and that's *very* tricky to hide! Sunshine, your magic makes you different and special, and I'd love you whatever magic you had."

"Really?" asked Sunshine hopefully.

"Really," said Evie firmly.

Sunshine buried her head in Evie's arms and Evie hugged her.

"Your hair, Evie!" gasped Ivy. She reached out and held up a strand of Evie's brown hair that had turned pink, turquoise and yellow. "You've bonded!"

Evie felt a rush of delight. "We're partners forever, Sunshine!"

"Partners and best friends," said Sunshine happily.

"Now let's use your awesome magic to help us get out of here," said Evie. "Can you blow a hole in the wall so we can escape?"

"I'll try," Sunshine said, tossing her mane. "Stand back, everyone, and watch out for flying stones."

Lyra put the new bit of map in her pocket with the original pieces. Everyone shuffled back down the passageway, leaving Evie alone with Sunshine by the closed-up entrance.

"What if I blow the whole tower to smithereens and hurt everyone?" asked Sunshine.

"You won't." Evie felt confident. "I know you're going to get your magic exactly right because you're the best, Sunshine!"

Sunshine took a deep breath and stamped her front hooves down hard. Bright pink sparks shot up in the darkness. There was a strong smell of burnt sugar and, as the sparks hit the stone wall, a deafening bang. The stones exploded outward in a cloud of dust, making everyone cough. Through the swirling dust, Evie saw Flash and Solomon, Dr Briar's unicorn, rearing backwards in surprise.

Dr Briar and Sam clung to their manes, struggling to keep their balance. The explosion seemed to have caught them in the middle of an argument.

Dr Briar spluttered. "You're not going to get away with this!" she shouted. "Give me the map!"

"No way!" yelled Lyra, galloping out on Misty. "Ruby dorm, back to the academy, NOW!"

CHAPTER TEN

Evie and Sunshine raced after their friends. "Are you OK?" Evie gasped to Sunshine. Magic was tiring for a unicorn when they first discovered their powers.

"I'm fine," said Sunshine. "I've already had quite a bit of practice at blowing things up!"

Evie hung on tightly to Sunshine's mane as they weaved through the trees. She could hear hooves pounding behind them. Glancing round, she saw Dr Briar coming up fast on Solomon with Sam and Flash a short way behind.

"Hurry, Sunshine!" Evie yelled.

Evie and Sunshine

Solomon reached Sunshine and pushed alongside her. Dr Briar leaned out to grab Evie's arm. "Give me the map!" she shrieked.

There was a sudden flash and a flurry of blue sparkles. Dr Briar's hand froze a millimetre away from Evie, and Solomon stopped as if suspended in time. Evie's and Sam's eyes met for a fleeting second. He nodded, as if urging her on.

"Go!" yelled Evie to Sunshine.

Sunshine's hooves thundered loudly as she galloped out of the trees. At the edge of the woods Evie glanced back. There was no sign of Dr Briar or Sam but she'd caught up with Misty, Sparkle and Flame. By the time they arrived back at the stables, all four unicorns were dripping with sweat, their sides heaving.

Evie's legs were like jelly as she slid from Sunshine and threw her arms round her neck. "I thought Dr Briar was going to grab me back in the woods."

"I can't believe Sam!" Sienna's eyes blazed. "He must have been in league with his aunt all along. He's a total snake!"

"No, he's not!" Evie protested. "He helped me escape just now." She told the others what had happened. "If Flash hadn't frozen time, Dr Briar would have pulled me off Sunshine."

Lyra frowned. "When we escaped, it looked like

Sam and Dr Briar were arguing. Maybe he was trying to stop her."

"Hmm," Sienna said, not looking convinced. "I still think he's a snake."

"Well, whoever's side he's on, the important thing is that we all got back safely," said Ivy.

"Should we tell the teachers what happened?" Evie asked.

"We'd get into really big trouble for sneaking out at night," said Sienna doubtfully.

"And they'd make us hand over the map, and then we wouldn't be able to find the treasure," said Lyra.

"Let's not tell!" they all said together.

They grinned at each other.

"So this stays as our secret," said Lyra.

Evie nodded. "We'd better watch out for Dr Briar though. She's not going to give up that easily. Hopefully, she won't try anything here at school though, not with the teachers so close by."

Lyra nodded. "We'll have to be extra careful. This next clue will lead us to the final piece of the map and then we can find the treasure!" She patted her pocket. "I'm not going to let any of the pieces out of my sight."

The girls hurried into the stables and fetched their unicorns buckets of sky berries. Evie tipped the berries into Sunshine's manger then kissed her on the muzzle. "Goodnight, Sunshine. See you tomorrow."

"Night, Evie." Sunshine blew her a kiss back, her dark eyes shining happily.

Evie's heart filled with joy. She was so glad she and Sunshine had sorted everything out. Now she had found her magic and they had bonded, they would definitely be graduating at the end of the year and be together forever.

"You know, I could always stay here in the stable with you tonight," said Evie, not wanting to leave.

"You mean have a sleepover?" said Sunshine in delight.

Lyra poked her head into Sunshine's stable. "A sleepover in the stables! That's a brilliant idea! We could all squeeze in here together."

"But what about Dr Briar?" said Evie, frowning. "She might try and attack us."

"Not with all the teachers' unicorns here," Lyra reassured her. "They'd raise the alarm in no time. I bet she won't try anything now we're back at school." She called to Ivy and Sienna. "What do you think about having a sleepover here tonight?"

The others agreed it was a great idea. While Ivy and Sienna fetched some warm rugs from the tack room, Lyra and Evie got some more straw and made Sunshine's bed super thick. Then they all squeezed inside. The unicorns lay down in the straw and the girls curled up next to them, covering themselves with the rugs and their unicorns' manes.

"Night, everyone," said Sienna, yawning sleepily.

One by one they fell asleep. Leaning her head against Sunshine's neck, and closing her eyes, Evie's heart swelled with happiness. She had the best friends in the world, a wonderful unicorn who loved her, and another adventure was waiting just round the corner.

"I'm so glad you're my partner, Evie," Sunshine murmured.

Evie smiled and snuggled closer. "And I'm so glad you're mine!"

PRINCESS of PETS

Animal adventures, friendship and a royal family! From the author of The Rescue Princesses.

Another MAGICAL series from Nosy Crow!

SNOW SiSTERS